A Magical Sturgeon

D1502063

A MAGICAL STURGEON

JOSEPH DANDURAND

ILLUSTRATIONS BY ELINOR ATKINS

NIGHTWOOD EDITIONS

2022

In the river sat a sturgeon, born there, so they say, thousands of years ago, though the sturgeon have been here for two hundred million years.

She was at first a little egg, born into the river. Now the sturgeon is back, but how did she get here? How did the first sturgeon come to be? Earth and river, moons and suns and clouds. Time, thousands of years, and the skwó:wech has seen it all. But what gift does this sturgeon have for us?

The story of this magical sturgeon begins near our village of Squa'lets, where waters divide. This is a place as old as the sturgeon.

How big is this sturgeon? She is well over one hundred pounds and about six feet long with old grey skin covering her still razor-sharp spines, some worn down by the years of brushing the bottom of this magnificent river's bottom. Her belly is smooth white and she has black eyes, these eyes of the sturgeon that love the day and love the night.

As the magical sturgeon swims along the shores of Squa'lets, two young Kwantlen girls, sisters, are told by their mother that they are to go to the river and take one sturgeon for their supper. Their mother also says that they are to leave something for the river. She gives them two big pieces of bread and two big pieces of smoked fish and tells them to throw the bread and the fish to the river once they have taken a sturgeon. They are to throw the food as an offering of thanks to the river for providing the family with a meal.

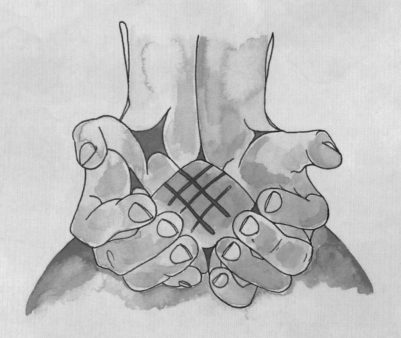

The sisters push their father's dugout canoe onto the water and begin to paddle out to the middle of the river. They have come to try to spear the giant sturgeon so they may bring the fish back to their village and feed everyone for the long winter ahead. They have come to spear the sturgeon, the magical sturgeon, the one that has become legend because it cannot be caught by anyone.

The two sisters sit in their dugout canoe and drop their spear into the water and let it touch the bottom of the river. They wait for the magical sturgeon to swim into the barbed hooks of the mighty spear made by their father.

Morning turns into midday and then into afternoon as both sisters begin to get hungry. They knew they must not eat the food offering because they must give it to the river when the river gives them a sturgeon.

They wait and wait until the older sister decides that she will just eat half of the food offering: one piece of the bread and one piece of the smoked fish. She begins to eat but the cries of her little sister are too much, so the older sister gives her little sister the other half of the food offering. They both sit there in their father's dugout canoe in the middle of the river with their spear sitting on the bottom waiting for the magical sturgeon to appear.

They both sit there, full-bellied and sleepy, when suddenly the spear is moving, as a large sturgeon becomes hooked down below at the bottom of the river.

Then the sturgeon takes off and begins to drag the boat and the two sisters downriver farther and farther away from their village of Squa'lets.

The older sister holds on to the canoe as best she can but her little sister cannot hold on any longer and she falls into the river just as the sturgeon begins to get tired. The older sister stands up and begins to pull the spear and the sturgeon into the dugout canoe. She paddles and paddles in search of her little sister but her little sister is gone. The older sister cries as she hears the river speak.

"Where is my food offering?"

Over and over the older sister can hear the river's words. She paddles back to their island and she walks into Squa'lets with the largest sturgeon ever seen. They say it is the magical sturgeon. They say it is the one that no one could catch. Everyone is happy and singing songs, and they begin to cut the magical sturgeon into pieces for all the families of the village. Everyone is happy except the older sister. She is sad because she did not offer the food to the river like she was told to do, and it was the river who had taken her little sister.

As the older sister sits there and cries for her lost little sister, a shxwlá:m or healer brings her the backbone of the magical sturgeon and tells her she must bring this to the river and give it back as an offering of thanks. The older sister does what she is told to do by the shxwlá:m. She walks down to the river and gets in her father's dugout canoe and paddles to the exact spot that she had speared the magical sturgeon. She paddles to the exact spot where the river had taken her little sister and she tosses the mighty backbone of the largest magical sturgeon back to the river.

As the bone falls to the bottom of the river, the older sister can hear her little sister's voice singing the song they always sang when they went fishing and when they went to the river to offer back the bones of the fish that they had been given by the river.

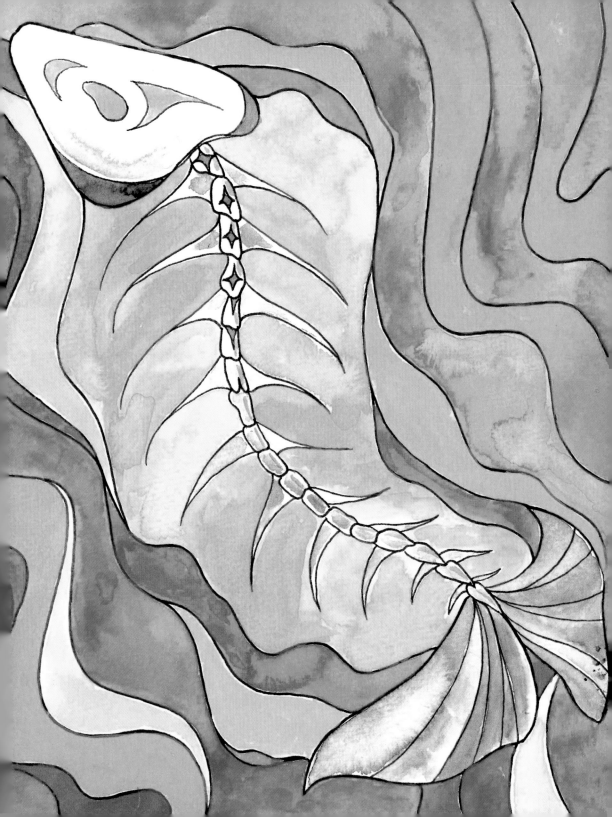

Hey ya hey ya yo yo hey,

Hey ya hey ya yo yo hey,

Ahey ya ahey ya,

Ahey ya ahey ya, hey!

She can hear her little sister singing their song! When the older sister looks up from the river, there on the shore is her little sister walking home, singing the song of thanks. The river has given her back as thanks for the offering of the bones, the bones of the magical sturgeon.

Copyright © Joseph Dandurand, 2022
Illustrations © Elinor Atkins, 2022

1 2 3 4 5 — 26 25 24 23 22

ALL RIGHTS RESERVED. No part of this publication may be reproduced, stored in a retrieval system or transmitted, in any form or by any means, without prior permission of the publisher or, in the case of photocopying or other reprographic copying, a licence from Access Copyright, the Canadian Copyright Licensing Agency, www.accesscopyright.ca, info@accesscopyright.ca.

Nightwood Editions
P.O. Box 1779
Gibsons, BC VON 1V0
Canada
www.nightwoodeditions.com

BOOK LAYOUT: Carleton Wilson

Canada

Canada Council   Conseil des Arts
for the Arts   du Canada

BRITISH COLUMBIA
ARTS COUNCIL

BRITISH
COLUMBIA

Nightwood Editions acknowledges the support of the Canada Council for the Arts, the Government of Canada, and the Province of British Columbia through the BC Arts Council.

This book has been produced on 100% post-consumer recycled, ancient-forest-free paper, processed chlorine-free and printed with vegetable-based dyes.

Printed and bound in Canada.

LIBRARY AND ARCHIVES CANADA CATALOGUING IN PUBLICATION

Title: A magical sturgeon / Joseph Dandurand ; illustrations by Elinor Atkins.
Names: Dandurand, Joseph A., author. | Atkins, Elinor, illustrator.
Identifiers: Canadiana (print) 20210396768 | Canadiana (ebook) 20210396830 |
ISBN 9780889713901 (softcover) | ISBN 9780889713918 (EPUB)
Classification: LCC PS8557.A523 M34 2022 | DDC jC813/.54—dc23